SUGAR DADDY

**Written & Un-Edited
by Darick Spears**

Sugar Daddy

ISBN: 978-1-954133-05-1

Published through

Darick Books

DDS MediaWorks LLC. / 21st Century Shakespears Publishing

www.darickbooks.com

Get Your Book Written & Published today

By

Darick Spears

Email: darick@ddsmediaworks.com

Call 414-988-4946

RELATIONSHIPS START OFF SO INNOCENT,
THAT IS UNTIL THE TOXINS KICK IN.
THE WORLDLY POLLUTANTS,
NECESSITY,
NECESSITY,
NECESSITY.
WHAT HAPPENS WHEN YOU HAVE TO DO WHAT'S NECESSARY TO SURVIVE?

TOM AND TINA WERE PRETTY CLOSE FRIENDS.
THEY HAD KNOWN EACH OTHER FOR MANY YEARS.
TOM WAS OLDER THAN TINA, AND HAD NOTHING BUT PURE LOVE FOR HER.
PROUD AS HE WATCHED HER GROW UP TO BECOME A VERY PRETTY WOMAN.

BUT AS TINA BECAME A WOMAN,
THE DYNAMIC OF THEIR
RELATIONSHIP BEGAN TO
CHANGE.
TOM STILL VIEWED TINA AS
THE YOUNG GIRL HE HAD
ALWAYS MENTORED.
THEY WERE CLOSE,
BUT SHE STARTED TO VIEW
TOM DIFFERENTLY.

SHE NOW HAD REAL RESPONSIBILITIES LIKE RENT, GROCERIES, AND STABILITY.
ASKING TOM FOR MONEY HERE AND THERE WAS NOT GOING TO HELP HER SITUATION,
SO SHE CONJURED UP ENOUGH NERVE TO PRESENT TOM WITH A PROPOSITION.

Tina asked Tom if he would buy her some lingerie?
He was totally against buying her lingerie so that she could wear it for the next person.
So, he only agreed to do it if she wore the lingerie for him as well.

TINA AGREED,
AND TOM BOUGHT HER THE OUTFIT.
IT WAS STRANGE AT FIRST,
BUT TOM AND TINA GOT USED TO IT.
SHE WOULD MODEL FOR HIM,
KISS HIM..
AND FLIRT HARDCORE.
BUT TINA HAD MORE NEEDS AND
KEPT PUSHING THE SUGAR DADDY
PROPOSAL.

SO, TOM TOLD TINA THAT IF HE BECAME HER SUGAR DADDY, THERE WOULD BE THINGS SHE WOULD HAVE TO DO IN RETURN.
HE TOLD HER HE WOULD COMPILE A LIST OF THINGS,
AND THEY WOULD HAVE TO COME UP WITH AN AGREEMENT.

Tina agreed.
But Tom was still a little
unsure of the matter.
They knew each other's
families and if things went
left -- some people could get
hurt.

Tina was in her 20's and had strong sexual energy. She would send Tom videos of her dancing, stripping, and more.
His lust for her was growing by the day.

TOM MADE IT A RULE THAT SHE HAD TO BE HIS SEX SLAVE, AS WELL AS HIS FULFILLER ON EVERY LEVEL.
IF SHE COULD DO THIS, THEN IN RETURN, HE WOULD BE HER SUGAR DADDY.

TINA AGREED,
AND THEY MADE LOVE DAILY.
TOM PAID TINA'S BILLS, BOUGHT
HER GROCERIES, CLOTHES, AND
MORE.

TOM AND TINA LOVED EACH OTHER, THEY WANTED THE BEST FOR ONE ANOTHER AND REMAINED VERY CLOSE. SO TINA DECIDED THAT SHE WOULD TELL HER GIRLFRIEND BECAUSE THE TWO OF THEM ALWAYS WANTED A CHILD. BUT SHE WOULD NOT MAKE TOM TELL HIS WIFE.

Tina and Tom would go on to have 2 children together. Tom would still assume the position of a Sugar Daddy. Money wasn't a thing for him,
He was a very successful Businessman.

TOM AND TINA HAD THE STRANGEST RELATIONSHIP, BUT THEY TRULY LOVED ONE ANOTHER.
TINA EVEN MARRIED HER GIRLFRIEND,
AND TOM DID NOT HAVE A PROBLEM WITH IT.

Tom continued to be there for Tina and their children.
No one knew about their secret relationship except for Tina's wife.
It's a crazy love story.

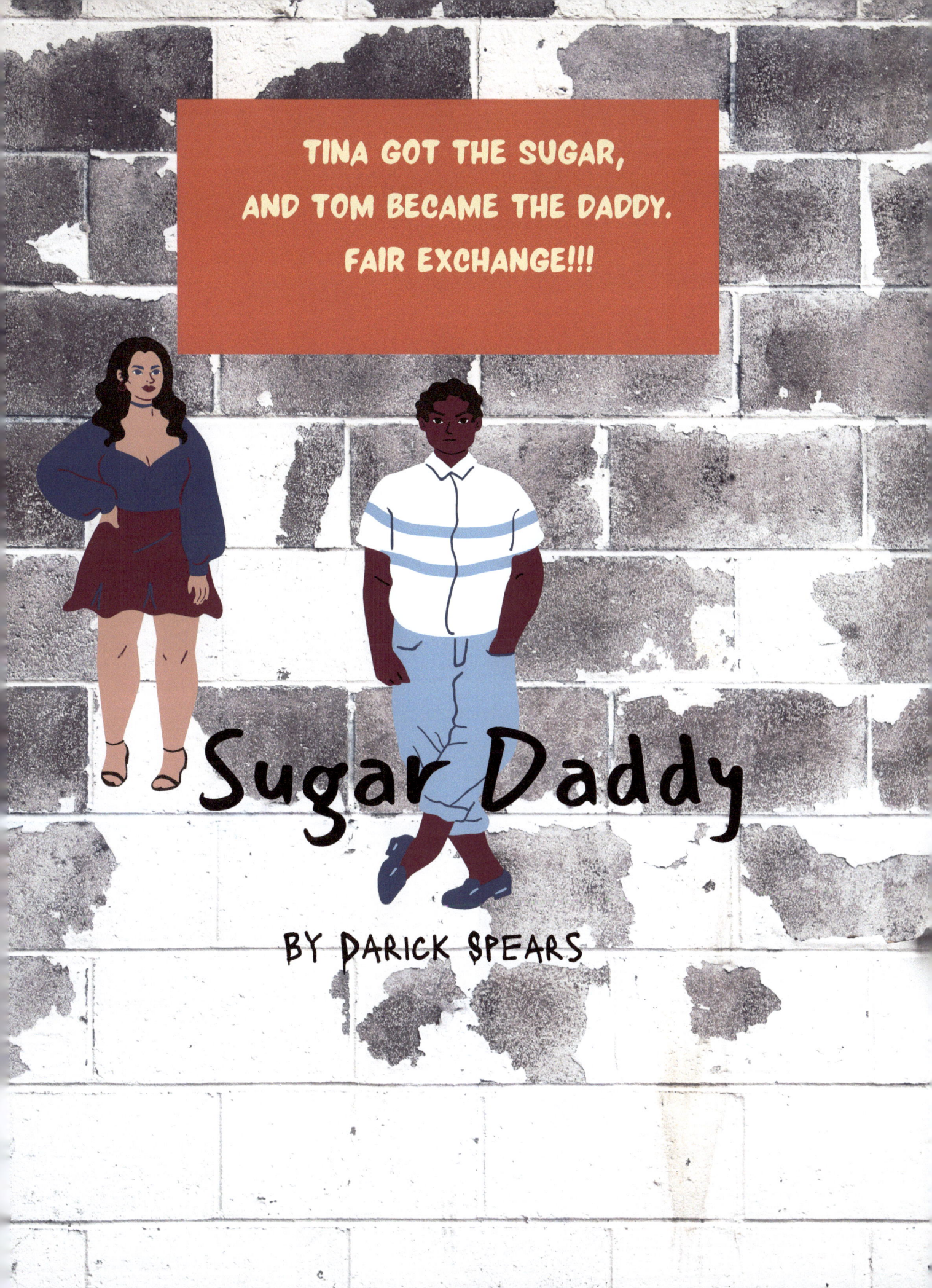

www.ingramcontent.com/pod-product-compliance
Lightning Source LLC
Chambersburg PA
CBHW041930010726

47507CB00003BA/235

Two friends, two propositions, and one agreement. But how far is she willing to go to get what she wants?

Darick Books 📚

www.darickbooks.com

ISBN 9781954133051

90000

9 781954 133051

Pimp Hard

DARICK SPEARS